Wild, Wild West

Wild, Wild West

Judy Delton

Illustrated by Alan Tiegreen

A Yearling Book

Published by
Bantam Doubleday Dell Books for Young Readers
a division of
Random House, Inc.
1540 Broadway
New York, New York 10036

Visit us on the Web! www.randomhouse.com
Educators and librarians, visit the BDD Teacher's Resource Center at www.randomhouse.com/teachers

ISBN: 0-440-41342-7

Printed in the United States of America

April 1999

10 9 8 7 6 5 4 3 2 1

CWO

Contents

For my dad and Craig Lien, the two
perfect fathers in my life

And for Sheila, of course

CHAPTER 1

Mood Goo and Eggy Rolls

"**W**hy do we have to take a make-believe trip?" snorted Sonny Stone. "I like real trips where we go on a jet or a train or a bus or something."

The Pee Wee Scouts were on the way to their Tuesday meeting at Mrs. Peters's house.

"That's all Mrs. Peters said last week, that our next badge was going to be for taking a make-believe trip somewhere," said Mary Beth Kelly. She was Molly Duff's best friend in the whole world.

"Make-believe can be fun," said Molly, although deep down she felt the same as Sonny. A real trip was better.

"Maybe it's to Duluth," said Tim Noon. "My uncle lives there. I think that's where Paul Bunyan and his blue ox live."

Rachel Meyers sighed. "That's not Duluth," she said. "That's Bemidji. That's where Paul Bunyan is. Or at least a big statue of him."

"Pooh," said Lisa Ronning. "Who wants to take a trip in Minnesota? We always do that because we live here."

Molly agreed. She wanted to go on a trip, make-believe or real, that would take them to faraway places.

"I'll bet it's Washington, D.C.," said Roger White. "Mrs. Peters likes all that government stuff, like presidents' houses and statues of Lincoln."

"Maybe we'll see George Washington's

wooden teeth!" said Tracy Barnes. "He really had wooden teeth, you know!"

"Teeth aren't made of wood," said Roger in disgust. "Our teeth are made out of plastic."

"Real teeth aren't plastic," said Lisa. "They grow in your mouth. They must be cement or something."

"George Washington's wooden teeth were false teeth," said Jody George, wheeling his chair faster to keep up with the other Pee Wees. "And you can't see them in Washington. They're probably buried with him at Mount Vernon."

"Maybe we're going to climb Mount Vernon!" said Tim Noon. "That's that real high mountain where everyone freezes and they end up having to eat one another!"

"Wow!" said Roger. "That sounds like a fun place to go!"

Rachel stamped her foot. "You guys are

so dumb!" she said. "Mount Vernon is not a mountain. It's the place where George Washington lived with his wife, Martha. The mountain you're thinking of is Everest."

"I'll bet Jody knew that," said Molly to Mary Beth. "But he never brags like Rachel."

"Well, anyone should know that Mount Vernon isn't really a mountain," said Mary Beth.

"I think they teach that in third grade," said Molly. "Not second." The Pee Wees were in second grade.

"Well, it's on TV," said Mary Beth. "On the History Channel."

"I don't think Tim watches the History Channel," said Molly. "He watches cartoons."

They both remembered how Tim had had a hard time getting his library badge because he couldn't read the books he'd taken out. Molly had helped him.

"Maybe," said Rachel, "we're going to China. Just pretend, of course. But it would be fun."

The Pee Wees thought about that.

"I like Chinese food," said Kenny Baker. Kenny was Patty's twin brother.

"Yuck! I don't," said Sonny. "I'm not going there and eating all those eggy rolls. And that mood goo noodles. Their food has baby-talk names. They don't even know how to pronounce stuff."

"You guys are so boring," said Rachel. "All you eat is American food, like hot dogs and peanut butter. Chinese food is gourmet."

No one had anything to say because no one but Jody knew what *gourmet* was. And he wouldn't show off by telling.

"Well, we'll find out today where we'll

be going," said Tracy when they got to Mrs. Peters's house.

Mrs. Peters was at the door with baby Nick. "Come on in!" she called, smiling.

Molly got goose bumps on her arms. She always did when a new badge was about to be announced. New badges were what the Pee Wees lived for. They were fun to earn and fun to collect. The Pee Wees had lots and lots of badges, but they never could have enough. A new badge was the most exciting thing that happened, except for Halloween and Christmas!

The Pee Wees followed Mrs. Peters down the basement steps. They hung up their sweaters and sat down around the long table where they had their meetings. In the middle of the table was a big statue of a horse with a cowboy on its back.

"What's that thing for?" asked Roger, pointing.

"Maybe it's just a decoration," said Lisa.

But Molly knew better. This horse meant something. Mrs. Peters didn't have decorations on the Pee Wees' table that didn't mean something. Were they going to study animals? Were they taking a trip to the zoo?

Sonny began to bang on the table with a library book. "Okay, what's the badge?" he said. "Do we have to eat eggy rolls to get it?"

"Are we going to climb a mountain?" asked Tim.

"Are we going to see George Washington's false teeth?" asked Tracy.

"I bet we're going to ride horses," said Jody, looking at the horse and cowboy.

"Jody is the closest," laughed Mrs. Peters. "Our new badge is going to be a Wild West badge. And I'm going to tell you all about it right now."

The Pee Wees cheered.

"Ride 'em, cowboy!" shouted Kenny.

CHAPTER 2

Westward, Ho!

"I love horses!" said Ashley, who was a cousin of the Baker twins. "When we're in California I belong to the Saddle Scouts. We ride all the time."

"Well, you'll be a big help," said Mrs. Peters. "You can give us firsthand information."

"I don't like cowboys and fences and cactuses and stuff," said Patty.

"Cacti," said Rachel. "The plural of *cactus* is *cacti*."

"Well, I still don't like them," said Patty.

"Boy, I do!" said Roger. He aimed an imaginary gun at Sonny and shouted, "Bang bang! You're dead!"

Sonny fell to the floor and played dead. Roger began chasing the other boys around the room, shooting and shouting.

Mrs. Peters clapped her hands.

"We can't really go as far west as I'd like," she said. "The real ranches are in Montana and Nevada. But we will do the next best thing. We are going to a dude ranch in South Dakota. It has cowboys and horses and roundups and even square dancing," she said.

"Then we're taking a real trip!" said Kenny.

The Pee Wees all cheered. The West might not be as wild in South Dakota as it was in Montana, but at least they wouldn't be looking at maps of China and eating phony Chinese food!

"A real cowboy from Montana started

the ranch. Now people take vacations there," Mrs. Peters continued. "We'll get to see what the West used to be like. And we have Lisa to thank for telling us about this place. The cowboy who runs it is a friend of her parents'."

Everyone stared at Lisa. No other Pee Wees knew real cowboys.

"We were there last summer," said Lisa. "It's really cool."

"I'm scared of horses," whined Sonny. "They have big noses when you get up close."

"Pooh," said Ashley. "Horses are friendly and kind. My horse at home is called Clover. He eats sugar lumps and carrots right out of my hand."

Molly liked horses. She remembered when the Pee Wees had been in a parade. Some of them had ridden horses then. But they were not galloping horses. They had walked slowly for a block or two. A man had led them and watched to make sure no one fell off. Western horses galloped. They did not walk in a street led by a man with a rope. Molly remembered how high off the ground it was on the back of a horse. It was a long, long way down. No doubt Lisa's cowboy had big horses without anyone to lead them.

Suddenly the Pee Wees heard someone sniffling. It was Tracy.

"I'm allergic to horses," she said. "I'll have to stay home!"

"I'm sure you can come," said their leader. "You just won't go in the barn or get near horses. There are lots of other things to do. There is a restored ghost town nearby to visit."

Tracy looked doubtful.

"Don't worry about anything," said Mrs. Peters. "Our last few badges were lots and lots of work. I thought it was time we just plain had fun."

"Yay!" cheered the Pee Wees. A badge without work always appealed to them. They were not lazy (except for Roger and Sonny), but they all liked the idea of fun.

"We'll talk more about the trip later," Mrs. Peters went on. "Today I'll just give you some background information about the Wild West. All you have to do is listen. It's good to know the basics before you start on a trip.

"The West is more than cowboys," she added.

"How about Daniel Boone?" asked Tim. "I saw him in a movie. He had one of those caps with a long tail on it."

"Raccoon," said Jody. "Those are raccoon caps."

"The Lone Ranger is from the West," said Roger.

"He's not even real," said Patty Baker. "He's just a movie character."

"He is too real!" said Roger.

Lisa rolled her eyes. Today Lisa was the expert. "He's no more real than Hopalong Cassidy or Superman."

Roger looked disappointed. He didn't want to think his heroes were make-believe.

"The West is also famous for gold mines," said Mrs. Peters. "When gold was discovered in Montana, many people from the East traveled west in covered wagons. They hoped to pan for gold and become rich. But not very many of them did. It was a long, hard trip across the prairie. There were no roads, and there were wild animals and Native Americans already living there."

The Pee Wees looked thoughtful. The West didn't sound like fun back then. There wasn't even a Disneyland to go to, thought Molly.

"Where's the West?" asked Sonny. "My mom says Minneapolis is west."

Some of the Pee Wees began to chuckle.

"Hey! Let's go to Minneapolis and dig for gold!" shouted Roger. "Giddyap!"

Molly didn't think they should laugh at Sonny's question. Probably lots of the Pee Wees didn't know where the West was. Molly knew California was west, but she wasn't sure what other states were out there, besides Montana and Nevada.

Ashley groaned. "I live in the West," she said. "California is as far west as you can go."

"Without falling in the ocean," said Kenny.

Mrs. Peters unfolded a map that was on the table. She held it up. "Here is where we are," she said, pointing to a spot in the middle and kind of high up. "This is Minnesota. This star is St. Paul. It's the state capital."

Mrs. Peters pointed to the states to the right of Minnesota.

"This is the East," she said. "Where the

16

sun comes up. All these states near the Atlantic Ocean were settled before Minnesota."

"Why?" asked Tracy. "Why didn't the people settle out West to start with?"

"Actually, they did," said Kevin. "My dad told me the Spanish came up from Mexico and built Santa Fe even before the Pilgrims landed at Plymouth Rock."

Molly was proud of Kevin. She wanted to marry him someday. Either him or Jody. Kevin was smart, and he wanted to be mayor when he grew up. Molly knew she would vote for him.

"That's true," said Jody. "But the people who started the United States were from England. So they settled in the part of the country closest to England."

"That's right!" said Mrs. Peters. "And for a long time, none of the immigrants could afford to go all the way across the United States. Besides, they didn't know

what was out there. It was scary. How would they find food and places to stay?"

"What's an immigrant, Mrs. Peters?" asked Tracy.

"Someone who comes from somewhere else," said Ashley.

Mrs. Peters nodded. Then she pointed to the rest of the map, to the states left of Minnesota.

"This is the West," she said. "California, Nevada, Montana, New Mexico, Arizona, and all these other states. This is where the pioneers went looking for gold. They had to cross the big, hot desert. When they ran out of water, some died of thirst." Mrs. Peters pointed to the big sandy-colored area on the map.

Tim's hand was waving. "Mrs. Peters, camels store water in their humps."

"But people don't," said Sonny.

"Cacti store water too," said Rachel. "But that won't save you in the desert."

"Everyone needs water," said their leader. "So not everyone made it all the way west. Some of the people stopped and settled along the way. They built homes, and little towns sprang up here and there. Some did not get any farther than Minnesota. To go all the way from New York to California took weeks, even months. Now it takes only a few hours in a plane. In those days, the way was long and bumpy and travelers were often cold and hungry. The trip is over three thousand miles."

The Pee Wees stared at the map. It was hard to believe a trip could take that long, thought Molly. It was only ten miles to Minneapolis. Imagine three thousand miles! And back then people didn't have cars.

"There were no movies in Hollywood then," said Mrs. Peters. "There wasn't even a Hollywood. From the Mississippi River to the Rocky Mountains was just wide open prairie. The Indians there were not happy that the pioneers were taking over their land."

This sounded like a sad story. And a sad badge to earn. The West didn't sound like a happy place to visit.

Molly felt like crying for the poor pioneers. And for the Indians who had had their land stolen. Today all people had to do for water was turn on the faucet. What if she had been born then? She could have died! Had her ancestors traveled west too? Maybe they only got as far as Minnesota and stayed there. Molly was glad they did. Otherwise they could have died in the desert looking for water. There must not have been grocery stores then. Where did the pioneers get food? This was not going to be a fun badge to earn. Even though Mrs. Peters had said it would be.

"When does this badge start getting to be fun?" asked Patty.

CHAPTER 3

Good News and Bad News

Mrs. Peters laughed. "It will be fun right away!" she said. "The trip will be fun. And staying overnight and sleeping in the bunkhouse like the cowboys do will be fun. We'll wear ten-gallon hats. We'll visit the ghost town. We'll learn how they round up cattle and do some lassoing ourselves."

The Pee Wees cheered. This was good news! This was the fun badge they'd been waiting for. No work involved.

The boys ran around pretending to lasso each other with imaginary ropes.

"And of course we'll ride horses and square-dance."

Now the Pee Wee cheers turned to frowns. Some of them began to boo. Dancing was definitely bad news.

"I can't dance, Mrs. Peters!" shouted Tim.

"Neither can we," said Kenny and Patty.

"But we'll learn!" said their leader.

Mary Beth groaned. "I thought we didn't have to learn anything," she said to Molly. "I thought it was just supposed to be fun! Learning to dance and ride horses sounds like work."

"Trust me," said Mrs. Peters. "It will be fun. Dancing is not only fun, it's good exercise. Just wait till you hear the fiddler play and you and your partner promenade in that big barn—"

"Partner?" shrieked Tracy. "Do we have to have boys for partners?"

"Well, yes, but . . ."

The Pee Wees were now moaning and groaning so loudly Mrs. Peters couldn't continue.

"I'm not dancing with Roger!" said Rachel, stamping her foot.

"Or Sonny," said Patty.

"It's fun," said Lisa. "You don't dance exactly *with* them. You make a big square and everyone dances together."

The Pee Wees looked doubtful. Together or not, if girls had to have boy partners it sounded grim, thought Molly. Horseback riding sounded grim too. It was fun only if you could stay on the horse!

"Rat's knees," she said. "I knew it was too good to be true."

Mrs. Peters went on to explain that they would leave early on Friday. Mr. Peters would drive the van with some of the Pee

Wees. The others would ride with Mr. and Mrs. Baker and Kevin's parents, who were coming along as chaperones. Lisa's mother would come too.

"We will stay two nights, camping in the bunkhouse like cowboys," Mrs. Peters said. "Cowboy Andy's ranch is called the Lazy T, just north of the ghost town called Bone Junction. The town was named for a pile of bones that was found there years ago. Perhaps some pioneers only got as far as South Dakota. Or maybe they were settlers who had some misfortune."

"Maybe they were dog bones," said Tim.

"Or squirrel bones," added Sonny.

"I hope they weren't people bones," said Patty. "That would be spooky."

"It was a long time ago," said their leader, who did not explain what kind of bones were found in Bone Junction. "We

may find some old arrowheads and arti-
facts ourselves," she added. "Once Bone
Junction was a thriving Western town."

"I have a list for all of you to give to
your parents," she went on. "It tells what
you need to bring, what time we leave and
return, and what we'll be doing at the
ranch each day. Be sure to give it to them,
and then it's Westward Ho! We'll be off to
be cowhands for the weekend!"

The Pee Wees cheered. Molly tried to
put the dancing out of her mind, and she
cheered too. After all, horses and a ranch
and a cowboy were bound to mean fun.
Maybe she could think of a way to get out
of square dancing. One thing was for sure.
She would have to do something drastic—
anything—to keep from dancing with
Sonny or Roger.

Rat's knees, having fun was a lot of
work.

When Molly got home, her mom looked at the list and got Molly's suitcase out of the attic.

"This sounds like so much fun!" she said. "I wish your dad and I could go along this time, but we have to work. We used to love to square-dance. 'Do-si-do and around we go. Swing your partner and dip down low!' "

Mrs. Duff had a faraway look in her eye as she danced around the room.

"I don't want to dance with Roger," said Molly.

"Pooh," said her mother, waving Molly's words away. "It doesn't matter who you dance with because you keep changing partners. And moving fast."

Molly hoped her mom was right. She usually was.

On Wednesday and Thursday Molly was busy getting ready to go. She packed her Western-looking jeans and her most

Western-looking jacket. Her mom put some snacks in and a little bracelet with horses and spurs on it. "I used to wear that when I went square dancing," she said.

Then she began to sing a country-and-western song about a lovesick cowboy. When Molly's dad came home he got into the spirit of things and joined in. Molly hadn't realized her parents knew so much about the West!

When Friday morning came, the Pee Wees piled into the cars and were off! Off to have fun without work, off to earn a badge, off to round up cattle and meet Cowboy Andy!

CHAPTER 4

Grabbing Some Grub

The Pee Wees cheered as they crossed the Minnesota–South Dakota border. They were in another state! This was a real trip after all, thought Molly. Even though South Dakota wasn't far from home.

Before long the highway turned into a small road. And then a smaller one. And then Kevin pointed to a sign by the side of the road that read: BONE JUNCTION. POPULATION 210. He shouted out his window, "We're here!"

"Two hundred people isn't very many," said Mary Beth to Molly.

"That's why it's a ghost town," said Molly. "Ghost towns only have ghosts, not real people."

"I'm scared of ghosts!" cried Tracy.

"So am I!" said Patty.

"These ghosts are friendly ghosts," said Mrs. Peters. Tracy and Patty didn't seem convinced.

Bone Junction did look spooky. Some of the sidewalks were wooden and there was a saloon like those in Western movies. Some of the buildings had peeling paint and doors falling off their hinges.

But some of the stores were open and doing business.

"Since Cowboy Andy opened the ranch, the ghost town is coming back to life," said Mr. Peters. "The tourists like to shop in ghost towns."

"We'll come back here later and look

around," said Mrs. Peters. "Right now Cowboy Andy will be looking for us."

And he was. The Pee Wees came to a long white fence that seemed to go on for miles. Finally they reached a huge gate with a big wagon wheel beside it. A sign overhead read LAZY T RANCH. The cars followed a long road to a big ranch house, with barns and open pastures behind it. Horses were eating grass.

Coming around the corner from one of the big barns was a cowboy! He was tall and he had on boots with spurs on them. He was also wearing chaps over his pants. They were like leather overalls but open in the back. They were made to wear while riding horses. The man had on a huge cowboy hat and a Western necktie made of a piece of string held together with a silver horse's head. It sparkled in the spring sun. The cowboy's skin was tanned even though it was only June.

"Howdy, folks!" he said. "You're just in time for chow!"

"That's dinner," said Lisa as the Pee Wees got out of the cars and the van.

Lisa's mother introduced Cowboy Andy to the Peterses, and the Bakers, and the Moes, and to all the Pee Wees.

"It'll take me a while to learn all your names. But we've got plenty of time out here in the West. Time lasts a lot longer in the wide open spaces!"

"How much longer?" asked Tim. "I told my mom I'd be home on Sunday!"

That set Cowboy Andy to laughing and laughing. When he laughed he said something like *hee haw* and pounded his knee.

"Isn't he cute?" whispered Ashley to Molly.

"Who?" asked Molly.

"Andy," said Ashley. "He's really cute!"

Andy was interesting and strong, thought Molly. And he smelled like

horses. But she didn't think he was cute. Babies and puppies were cute. Not cowboys.

Molly told Mary Beth what Ashley had said.

"That's dumb," said Mary Beth. "He isn't going to be her boyfriend or anything. My mom says we're too young to think about boyfriends. He's probably married anyway."

But Ashley didn't seem to mind. She kept her eyes on Andy.

All of a sudden there was the sound of a bell ringing very loudly. It was so loud that the Pee Wees covered their ears.

"That's the old dinner bell," said Andy. "You never want to go too far away to hear that sound!"

"You couldn't," said Rachel. "It's loud enough to hear in St. Paul!"

"We'll serve us up some grub," said

Andy, "and after dinner we'll have a look around the place."

The Pee Wees washed up in bathrooms near the dining hall. On one of the bathroom doors there was a picture of a girl in a skirt swinging a lasso. On the other door there was a figure in chaps.

"That means *boys* and *girls*," said Lisa.

"Why don't they just say that?" asked Tracy.

The smells in the dining room were wonderful! Molly felt very hungry.

"It's the ranch air," said Mr. Peters, rubbing his stomach. "It makes you famished! Just wait till we ride horseback and do some work around the place. We'll be twice as hungry!"

The Pee Wees got in line at a long buffet table. It was loaded with food. Hot dogs and buns and potatoes and pickles. Ham and eggs and biscuits and honey and butter. Salads and carrot sticks and radish roses. Pancakes and maple syrup and grilled cheese sandwiches. Bacon and fruit of all kinds. At the head of the table stood the camp cook in a big white hat, serving things they couldn't help themselves to. There were a few other guests in line too. Most were wearing cowboy boots. Molly noticed that Lisa and her mom were sitting next to Cowboy Andy. Ashley was sitting on the other side of him.

"Dig in!" shouted Andy. "Grab some of those spuds. They'll stick to your ribs while you're working this afternoon! We got to lasso us some of those calves!"

The Pee Wees dug in. "Do we really have to catch calves?" asked Sonny.

"I think I'll start you nice and easy," said Andy, chewing on an ear of buttered corn. "We'll practice lassoing a post or two and see how you do."

Roger and Kevin and Kenny went back

for seconds. Then all the Pee Wees went back for strawberry shortcake for dessert. Ashley brought Andy some shortcake.

"If those pioneers had had all this food, they wouldn't have starved to death," said Tracy.

It made Molly sad to think of that. Why did they have so much, when those people long ago had had so little? It didn't seem fair. Molly was glad she was not a pioneer.

After lunch the Pee Wees helped clear the tables and carry the dishes to the kitchen. Kevin even helped one of the cowboys sweep the dining hall floor.

"We all like to pitch right in around here," said Andy.

"I love to pitch in," said Ashley.

When the work was done, the Pee Wees had a tour of the ranch. They saw the barns, the pens, the bunkhouse where they would sleep, and the silo that stored the hay and other food for the animals. Then they saw the ranch house, which had a fire blazing in the hearth and comfortable leather chairs to stretch out in. Andy showed them the rings where he exercised the horses and the fields where they ran. He showed them where they would have a bonfire and sing-along.

"And here is the barn where we square-dance!" said Andy. "Up there on that stool is where the fiddler sits. And the caller stands there with the microphone." He pointed.

A shiver went over Molly's skin. Not only did she not want to dance with boys, she didn't know *how* to dance! She wondered if any of the other Pee Wees did. She knew Lisa knew all about it.

"We'll have a little contest on Sunday for the best dancer," said Andy. "And that dancer will get a pretty little prize!"

Well, Molly knew one thing for sure. It wouldn't be her! No one could learn to dance well enough to win a prize in just two days. What was Mrs. Peters thinking, getting the Pee Wees into this? It would be embarrassing!

"Okay!" said Cowboy Andy. "Let's get you guys outfitted in ranch clothes so we can do some lassoing! All in favor, say *aye!*"

"Aye!" yelled the Pee Wees. They were off to be cowhands!

CHAPTER **5**

Roping and Riding

The Pee Wees followed Andy to a big room in the ranch house filled with cowboy boots and hats and other Western wear. It wasn't a store where you could buy things. It was a closet where guests could borrow things if they didn't want to buy them. A man named Chip helped the Pee Wees find their sizes. He measured their feet and tried hats on them until he found something that fit just right.

"I want this one!" shouted Sonny. He grabbed a hat off the shelf and put it on his head. The hat fell down over his eyes and rested on his nose. Everyone began to laugh.

"Hey, your head is too small!" shouted Roger.

Chip shook his head. "The hat's too big," he said. "Those are for adults."

Molly saw the hat she wanted. It was soft gray with a cord that went under your chin and a red bead you pushed up to keep the cord in place.

"That's so it won't fall off when you ride horseback or square-dance," said Chip.

Not *when* I square-dance, thought Molly. *If.*

Mary Beth chose a tan hat that fit her perfectly. "You look like a real cowgirl!" said Molly.

When they got their boots on, they really looked Western!

"Holy smokes!" said Andy. "You guys are the real McCoy!"

Mrs. Peters explained that he meant they looked like real cowboys.

The boots felt stiff on Molly's feet. It wasn't easy to walk at first. Before long, however, the Pee Wees got used to their new clothes and loped along behind Andy. Kevin and Kenny had very large boots. They were big boots for second-graders, thought Molly. Sonny and Tim and Rachel had the smallest ones.

Once on the range, Andy showed them how to lasso. He showed them how to hold and wind the rope. Then he taught them how to swing it sideways so it slipped through the air like a Frisbee and settled around a big fence post.

"I want to lasso a cow!" shouted Roger. "That's what cowboys do. They don't lasso a post!"

"He'll be lucky to get the post!" said Tracy. "He sure couldn't lasso a moving cow!"

Sure enough, when it was Roger's turn he missed the post and lassoed a bush! Sonny was next. He lassoed some blades of grass.

Kenny lassoed one of Andy's feet.

"Hold the rope loosely in your hand," Andy said. "Just relax."

That worked much better. But still no one was able to lasso the post. Andy let them move up closer for the second try, then even closer for the third.

"Pretty soon we'll be able to reach out our hand and grab that post!" said Rachel. "I don't think cowboys get this close to those calves."

At last, one of the Pee Wees succeeded! It was Patty! Everyone cheered and hooted, and Mr. Moe patted her on the back. "Good work, Patty!" he said.

Andy gave Patty a tiny lasso made of white rope, with a pin on the back. She put

it on her shirt. Everyone looked envious, especially the boys. And Ashley.

"I just need more practice," grumbled Roger.

"Sure," scoffed Rachel.

"So much for lassoing," said Andy. "Let's move on to the riding range."

Molly's heart skipped a beat. Lassoing was a snap compared to staying on the back of a bucking bronco.

Maybe she should get busy and think about how to get out of this. But she might not be able to avoid both riding *and* dancing. She'd have to choose one, or her leader would be suspicious. Which would be worse—falling off a horse or dancing with Roger? She knew the answer immediately. Dancing with Roger. She'd take her chances on horseback.

When they got to the stables, they met a cowboy named Bing. He was playing the guitar and singing a song about buffalo.

The horses were lined up, waiting. They were wearing saddles and pawing the ground with their hooves. Molly wished she had allergies like Tracy, who was sitting on a fence a long way from the horses. How lucky she was! Tracy would never have to learn to ride a horse.

Chip and Andy talked about riding safety. Then they showed the Pee Wees how to mount a horse.

"You put one foot here in the stirrup and swing your other leg up and over the saddle." Both cowboys demonstrated. "On," they said. "And off."

"I don't need any help, Andy," said Ashley. "I belong to the Saddle Scouts. We ride all the time. Maybe I can help you with the others."

But Andy didn't appear to need help.

Since the Pee Wees were so short, the cowboys had to hoist them up so they could get their feet in the stirrups.

"These are very gentle horses," said Chip. "Look how glad they are to see you." He fed one of the horses a carrot.

Molly did not think her horse looked glad to see her. He turned his huge head around and stared at her. He was not smiling. He was chewing and frowning and swishing his tail.

"They do that to get the flies off," said Lisa.

As the other Pee Wees sat on their horses, afraid to move, Ashley and Rachel gave theirs a slap on the back and said, "Giddyap!" Off they went down the bridle path! Rachel's hair was flying, and so was the tail of her horse. It looked like fun, but it looked scary.

"The rest of us are rookies," said Mr. Moe, "so we'll take our time."

"We'll just sit here awhile and get the feel of the beast," said Mrs. Moe.

Molly had the feel of the beast. It felt scary and high, as if she could slide off the saddle at any moment.

"Where are our seat belts?" shouted Tim. "We can't ride without seat belts. It's the law."

"I wouldn't mind having an air bag in front of me," said Kenny.

Neither would Molly. She wished she were sitting in a car seat, all strapped in, with an air bag protecting her.

"Why don't they build saddles like our recliner chair at home?" asked Mary Beth. "This isn't very comfortable."

One by one the Pee Wees rode off slowly on their horses. Chip showed them how to move to the rhythm of the horse's body.

"What if he runs?" shrieked Patty.

"He won't," said her mom. "Just try to relax and enjoy the ride."

51

Up ahead, Molly noticed Sonny slipping sideways in his saddle. Andy saw him too. By the time Sonny was about to slide to the ground, Andy was there to catch him. The cowboys were keeping a good watch on the Pee Wees. Sort of like lifeguards.

Lisa was slipping too. But she didn't fall off. She hung on and was very brave, thought Molly.

Sonny was riding on Chip's horse now. They were sharing a saddle.

"He cried so hard when he fell off, he wouldn't get back on his horse," said Mary Beth. "I don't think it's right for a baby like him to get to ride with the cowboy."

Sonny had a smirk on his face. It was as if he were saying, "Ha ha, look at me!"

Mary Beth was right. Sonny should not get rewarded for being a baby.

When the riding time was up, nobody

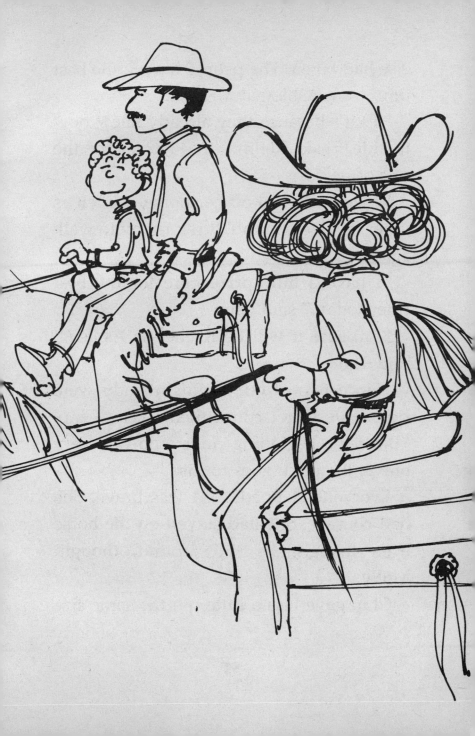

else had fallen. The people having the best time were Ashley and Rachel.

"That's because they already knew how to ride," said Kenny. "It's harder for the rest of us."

When Molly got off her horse, she felt as if her feet were numb! It felt funny to walk again!

"I have a little prize here for the best rider today," said Chip.

"I'm sure it will be Rachel or Ashley," said Tim.

"Since two of our Scouts already were riders, we won't count them," said Chip. "But for a beginning rider who was very brave, the prize goes to Lisa."

Everyone clapped. Lisa was brave. She had courage. She had stayed on the horse even though she slid around, thought Molly.

Chip gave Lisa a little pin the same size

as Patty's lasso pin. This one had a wire horse on it.

"I rode just as well," said Roger. "And I didn't get a prize."

"He's so selfish," said Mary Beth. "He's never happy for anyone else to win. He has to win at everything."

Well, Molly might not have won the prize, but she had ridden the horse and she had stayed on his back! And the best part was, riding the horse was over and she wouldn't have to do it again. Now, if she could just find some way out of tomorrow's square dance.

CHAPTER 6

Next Stop,
Bone Junction

"**L**et's all wash up and take a little trip into Bone Junction!" said Mr. Baker. "We have just enough time before supper. Andy is busy, but Chip said he'd come with us and show us the town."

Molly changed her T-shirt and brushed her teeth. She combed her hair and tied a Western bandanna in it. She was ready to see her first ghost town!

The Pee Wees piled into the cars and set off. When they got to Bone Junction, the wind was blowing and howling around the empty wooden buildings. Chip explained how the town had been settled. He explained that when there was no more work and no gold, the settlers had moved on and left behind the bare bones of the village. He showed them the old mill, the old saloon, and the old drugstore. Some of the stores were open again, but they still looked old. The people who worked in them were dressed up in old-fashioned clothes.

In the saloon, there were sawdust and peanut shells on the floor. Chip bought the Pee Wees glasses of soda pop and some popcorn. There was a man with a camera taking old-time photos. Some of the Pee Wees put on frontier costumes and had their pictures taken. When they finished, Mr. and Mrs. Baker said, "Now we think it will be fun to take a stroll around the town. You can visit the old post office and see the barns where they kept the horses. There were no cars back in the old days, so horses and stagecoaches served as transportation. One of the old stagecoaches is in the barn across the street. You can even climb into it if you're careful. We'll be right there watching. Call us if you need us."

Molly, Mary Beth, Tracy, and Patty went off toward the town square.

"I wonder where those bones Mrs. Peters told us about are," said Patty.

"I hope we don't see them," said Tracy.

But Molly and Mary Beth had the urge to look for the bones. They looked in the town fountain and under it. They looked under the wooden sidewalks. They looked in some of the empty lots, kicking their way through patches of tumbleweed.

"Let's go look at the stagecoach in the barn," said Patty.

"I can't go in barns," said Tracy.

"There are no horses in the barn anymore," said Mary Beth. "I don't think the stagecoach will make you sneeze."

The girls walked down the road to an old red barn. Molly pulled open a rickety, creaking door. There were cobwebs on all the windows, and it was dark inside. The girls crept in slowly, walking on tiptoe. The stagecoach was in the middle of the barn. It smelled like old leather. The stuffing was coming out of one of the seats, and one of the wheels was broken. The girls climbed on board.

"Real people rode in this once," whispered Tracy. "They're all dead now."

Molly got a shiver down her spine. Rat's knees, this was scary.

"What's that over in the corner?" said Mary Beth, pointing under one of the dirty barn windows.

The girls stared where she pointed.

Patty squinted. "It looks like a pile of old wood," she said.

"Or a pile of old bones!" said Tracy.

"It *is* bones!" shouted Mary Beth, who had run over to look.

Suddenly they heard a squealing noise overhead in the rafters. Something was up there! Something was on the floor too! It ran quickly between the girls' legs and disappeared.

"Yikes!" said Molly. "There's a ghost in here! This place is haunted!"

The girls were too scared to move. "He'll chase us!" said Tracy. "Let's just stand still till he goes away."

The squealing continued. Then something began to rustle and bang.

"I'm scared," cried Patty. "I want to get out of here!"

But when the girls began to run, they tripped over each other and fell to the floor. A loose board gave way. Before they knew it, Tracy was gone!

"Where is she?" shouted Patty.

"I wish there was a light in here!" said Mary Beth.

"Tracy!" shouted Molly. "Where are you?"

A muffled voice came from beneath them.

"I fell down here!" Tracy called.

The girls ran over to the spot where the voice came from. They discovered that the loose board was really a trapdoor in the floor. Tracy had fallen through.

The hole wasn't deep, but it was scary. Molly and Mary Beth reached down and pulled Tracy up onto the floor again. Tracy sneezed.

"There's hay down there!" she said. "I fell onto a pile of it!"

"That's the good news," said Patty. "It

broke your fall. The bad news is you're allergic to hay."

Suddenly the door of the barn opened wide. Sunlight shone in on the girls and the stagecoach. Mary Beth shrieked as a tiny mouse ran across her foot.

"What are you girls doing?" called Lisa's mom.

"We rode in the stagecoach," said Mary Beth.

"We found some bones," said Molly.

"I fell through the floor," said Tracy.

"We thought this place was haunted. But it may have been just a mouse," said Patty.

"I think you scared whatever ghosts or rodents there were away with your racket," said Lisa's mom. "There's no one here now but us!"

The girls brushed themselves off, and Mrs. Ronning examined the bones. "This is just a pile of branches," she said. "I think all the bones in Bone Junction are long gone!"

"So are we!" said Mary Beth, running out the door into the daylight. "Haunted or not, I've had enough of ghost towns for a while!"

CHAPTER 7

Trouble
in the Night

On the way back to the ranch, all the
Pee Wees talked at once about Bone Junction.

"I wish we lived here," said Tim. "There
are no schools in this town, not one!"

"A ghost town doesn't need a school,"
said Roger. "Ghosts don't go to school."

"I wouldn't want to live here," said
Jody. "It would be lonely. I'll bet in winter
there's no one in town."

Molly was surprised to hear Jody say

there was something he didn't like. Jody always found something nice to say about everything. He was the only Pee Wee who did that.

As if he could read Molly's thoughts, Jody said, "But it would probably be really pretty in winter with everything covered with snow. And we could take sleigh rides."

That's more like Jody, thought Molly.

When they got back to the ranch house, they were hungry. They had some chow in the dining hall, then got ready to turn in early for the night. They had done a lot in their first day. Tomorrow was the Day for Trouble, Molly reminded herself. She had to do some pretty heavy thinking about how she was going to escape square dancing. She needed a plan that would fool Mrs. Peters.

"Follow me," said Andy to the boys. "This room in the bunkhouse is for the men. Mrs. Peters and Mrs. Moe will take the ladies next door."

Molly hardly had time to look around the bunkhouse, she was so tired. She just brushed her teeth, climbed into her sleeping bag, and fell asleep. Mary Beth was chattering away about the ghost town and the dance tomorrow, but Molly didn't hear a thing. She was out like a light.

Molly had a dream about Sonny tripping her on the dance floor. She sat up in bed so fast she bumped her head on the bunk above her!

Just then, there was a piercing scream in the dark. *Yeeee owww!* It was right outside the bunkhouse window! Every girl in the room leaped out of bed.

"What is it?" screamed Patty. "What's out there?" The leaders got up and put on their robes. They listened carefully. Even Mrs. Peters looked scared, thought Molly.

Mrs. Baker went and looked out the

window. She reached through the opening and grabbed something.

"It's going to eat her!" screamed Tracy. "It's a monster! We have to save her!"

The thing Mrs. Baker grabbed began to screech even more loudly. The voice sounded familiar. Mrs. Baker leaned out the window and said, "Is that you, Sonny Stone?" She shook the thing by its hair.

"Owww," said Sonny. "Let go! Rog dared me to scare you guys. I had to do it."

"Creep," said Rachel in disgust.

All of a sudden a loud scream came from another direction. Sonny was in the doorway now, so it wasn't him!

Yeeee owww! screamed something very close to the bunkhouse.

"It's probably Roger," said Ashley. "Let's go back to bed."

But Roger was at the door rescuing Sonny! It wasn't Roger *or* Sonny.

"It's a monster!" cried Mary Beth. "It's one of those Western things, like a snake with horns or something!"

"Maybe it's a bear!" said Molly. Her hands were shaking. "They go looking for food at night in cabins and tents."

"Andy will save us," said Ashley. "Where is he?"

"I'm scared!" cried Sonny, putting his head in Mrs. Baker's lap. "It's going to get us!"

"Baby!" said Mary Beth. "It would serve him right if it did get him!"

Then doors began to bang in the ranch house.

"It's coming to get us!" screamed Sonny. "Get me out of here!"

He tore away from Mrs. Baker and dashed out the door.

Yeeee owww! came the monster's noise again. And this time for sure it wasn't Sonny.

Andy burst through the door. Ashley threw herself into his arms. "I knew you'd rescue us," she said. Andy just laughed. "No need to panic," he said. "It's just a coyote. We have lots of them out here in the Wild West!"

A coyote! Molly remembered they looked like big dogs or wolves. She had seen them in movies and books, howling at the moon. This was a real honest-to-goodness one, right here at the ranch!

"They make a lot of noise," said Chip, who had joined them. "But they don't bother us. Lots of animals live around here, roaming the plains."

Mrs. Peters got the girls back into their bunks and turned out lights. "Sleep tight," she said.

But for a long time no one could. Molly lay listening to the coyote as the moonlight filtered through the window. She gave a shiver. At last she fell asleep.

When she woke up, the sun was shining, and everyone else was still sleeping. It was very quiet. The only sound was the chatter of birds. Far away, a rooster was crowing. This was different from living in a city. Living in a city meant hearing buses and cars and trolleys and people's voices day and night. Jody was right. It was peaceful and pretty out here on the range.

Molly got up and crept to the door. She went outside and sat on a bench beside the bunkhouse. There were chipmunks looking for seeds. A small garter snake slithered by. The sun was warm and bright. This would be a nice place to live, thought Molly. Or it would be, if you didn't have to square-dance! That was the only bad news!

One by one the sleepy Pee Wees awoke and came outside to sit with Molly.

By the time Mrs. Peters and Mrs. Baker

and the cowboys came along, they had all dozed off in the sun.

"Up and at 'em!" called Andy, clapping his hands. "No time to nap in the sun! We have an old-fashioned barn dance to get ready for!"

Rat's knees! Those were words Molly didn't want to hear. What a way to ruin a fine day!

As they dressed and went in for breakfast, Molly tried to think how she could avoid dancing. What could possibly be her excuse? It would have to be something pretty convincing to fool Mrs. Peters. Their leader was used to the Pee Wees' tricks. She often said, "I have to get up pretty early in the morning to stay ahead of my Pee Wees."

Well, Molly should have gotten up a lot earlier to get ahead of Mrs. Peters! Between breakfast and dance time, there was a lot of work to do!

Molly didn't join in the breakfast conversation. Her mind was spinning with ideas. Should she develop a stomachache? Maybe if she ate too many pancakes she would have a real one! She didn't want to lie, and she didn't want to be sick, but anything would be better than dancing with Sonny or Roger.

She felt her forehead, the way her mother did when she wasn't feeling well. It was cool. No fever. Nature was not helping. She was going to have to do it alone.

She didn't want to catch anything bad enough to be taken to the hospital.

And she didn't want anything that needed special effects, like crutches, because she didn't have any.

She could lose her voice, but that wouldn't mean she couldn't dance.

This was a tricky situation.

All of a sudden she thought of an answer. Something that was bound to work.

CHAPTER 8

Do-si-do
and Around You Go

After breakfast some of the Pee Wees went horseback riding. Some of them went for a hike. And some of them gathered in the barn to help put up decorations for the big square dance. A man called Mr. Roscoe was there, showing people the dance steps. Molly sat down to watch. It wouldn't hurt to watch. As long as she didn't have to dance. In the first place, she didn't know how to. In the second place, she was definitely not going to be partners with Roger or Sonny.

"There is nothing as fun as square dancing!" shouted Mr. Roscoe. "It gets your blood moving and your feet tapping. And it's good exercise!"

A woman stood at his side. It must be Mrs. Roscoe, thought Molly. And she was right.

"My wife will help me demonstrate the steps," Mr. Roscoe said. "First of all, square dancing is done by groups of eight people. Four boys and four girls."

Ah, that was exactly the part Molly did not like!

"Each couple stands facing the center of an imaginary square. The dancers follow the directions of a caller. The caller shouts out the steps. I'll be the caller at your dance this afternoon. First, I may say 'Honor your partner.' That means you turn toward your partner. The boy bows and the girl curtsies."

He turned toward Mrs. Roscoe and bowed. His wife held her skirt out and curtsied.

"That's dumb!" Molly heard a voice say at the back of the room. It sounded like Roger.

"Then I might call 'Circle to the left,' " said Mr. Roscoe. "That means all eight of you join hands and move in a circle."

Join hands! With Sonny and Roger? Rat's knees. Molly wouldn't.

Now Mr. Roscoe had some people get on the stage and make a square. "When the caller says 'Do-si-do,' you face your partner and walk forward past your partner's right shoulder. Then you step to the right and walk backward past your partner's left shoulder. You end up facing each other again."

The people on the stage tried this. Some did it well, others got mixed up and ended up in the wrong position.

Now Mr. Roscoe was calling things like "Allemande left" and "Promenade home."

Molly watched as they did the Texas star and something called the rollaway half sashay. Pretty words, but Molly didn't want to hear any more of them. She got up and left. She headed back to the bunkhouse to think about how to escape this afternoon's dance session. Mary Beth and Tracy were in the bunkhouse too. No one said much. Suddenly Lisa burst in and said, "It's almost time for our lessons! We don't want to be late!" She looked at her watch.

"Some of the boys are over there already getting pointers," she added. "I saw Jody and Kevin going in."

"I've been there already," said Molly.

The other three girls yawned. "I'm too tired," said Tracy.

Molly and Mary Beth nodded. They felt tired too. Tired of worrying about dancing, thought Molly.

Lisa stamped her foot. "Come on, you guys! This will be fun! I want to win the prize for the best square dancer. Don't you?"

"I don't know how to dance," said Mary Beth.

"You'll learn," said Lisa. "That's why we're going over there now to practice. The big dance isn't until tonight."

Lisa got her square-dance skirt out of her suitcase and put it on. She twirled in a circle and it stood out all around her. With her little white boots, she looked just like a Western cowgirl, thought Molly. Molly wished she looked like that. But she didn't. And she didn't have a twirly skirt.

Molly decided it was time to put her

plan for avoiding square dancing into practice. She ran to the closet where the cleaning supplies were stored. Inside were lots of rags used for washing windows. Nobody would notice if Molly borrowed a few. She would return them tonight.

Molly picked out the biggest, longest white rags and went into the bathroom, locking the door behind her. She wrapped the rags around her leg from her ankle to her knee. She tied the ends and tucked them under. When she looked in the mirror, her rags appeared to be a giant bandage. Just what she wanted! She would have a broken leg. Or maybe just a sprained ankle. If it was broken she couldn't walk on it. And she had to walk. But she needed to practice limping so that it looked real. She limped around the bathroom, back and forth, until she could do it well.

She was ready to go. Surely no one

would expect her to dance now! With a leg as sore as this! As Molly started for the barn, she found she had no trouble limping. Her leg really did ache. She must have tied the bandage too tight. It felt as if her leg really was sprained!

When Molly arrived at the barn, Mr. Roscoe was just arranging some of the Pee Wees into squares. There were only a few Scouts there—Lisa and Jody and Kevin and Ashley. Ashley was busy trying to get Andy to be her partner. Where were the other Pee Wees?

Just as Molly was about to tell Mrs. Peters how sorry she was that she had to miss out on the dancing, Mary Beth came through the door with a cane! She was leaning on it, and she seemed to be crying. "I've got a sore foot. A horse stepped on it," she said.

Mary Beth had not told Molly, her best

friend, about this! It must have just happened!

Mary Beth sat down, and the door opened again. Tracy came in with red dots all over her face. "I've got an allergy," she said. "I can't dance because I'm itching."

Poor Tracy! Was she allergic to some weed that grew on the ranch?

The next Pee Wees to come in were Roger and Sonny. They had black patches over their eyes.

"I can't see!" said Sonny, walking around with his hands out, bumping into things. "I can't dance. I'm blind!"

"So am I," said Roger, bumping into Sonny and falling onto the floor.

Rat's knees, thought Molly. What is going on? Why was everyone in some kind of trouble?

Mrs. Peters suddenly began to laugh.

"All right!" she said. "You aren't fooling me! Not one of you!"

"I do itch!" shouted Tracy.

"And I'm blind," said Sonny.

Molly didn't say anything. Everyone had ruined her plan. They each had a plan of their own that was the same as hers! Had they copied her?

"I think we should talk about this," said Mrs. Peters.

"Well, I don't want to dance," said Roger, pulling off his eye patch. "I'm not dancing with Molly, I'll tell you that."

What a surprise! Roger did not want to dance with *her*! She wouldn't have to worry about dancing with him. Or Sonny, for that matter.

It seemed that everyone had the same problem. The girls didn't want a boy partner. (Especially Sonny or Roger.) And the boys didn't want girl partners.

"How about," said their leader, "having

the girls be partners with girls at first, and the boys with boys? Will that make you feel better?''

The Pee Wees thought about it. It wasn't perfect, but it would do for now.

"I don't like dancing, period," said Tim.

"You guys are so . . . dull!" said Rachel. "You don't like any new stuff!"

The Pee Wees reluctantly lined up. Mary Beth was Molly's partner, and that wasn't bad. It almost felt like fun.

Mr. Roscoe went through the steps again. The Pee Wees followed him in slow motion. "We'll play the music very slowly at first," he said, "so you can get the feel of it."

The music began. The Pee Wees paid close attention to Mr. Roscoe's words. They tried to do what he said. Most of the time they ended up backward or in another square or bumping into one another.

"Mr. Roscoe, Sonny is stepping on my feet!" yelled Tim.

"He stepped on mine too!" said Kenny. "I don't want to dance with him!"

"That's all right," said Mr. Roscoe. "That happens at first. By tonight, you'll be old pros."

The fiddler played and Mr. Roscoe sang. "Grab your sweetheart, give her a swing. Now promenade around that ring!"

"Isn't it fun when you do it right?" cried Mary Beth.

It was. The Pee Wees were all out of breath, but they were having fun! It was more like a game than it was like dancing. You had to think hard to do the right step at the right time. And by the end of the afternoon, the boys had girls for partners and no one minded. Not even Molly!

But of course her partner turned out to be Kenny. She liked Kenny, and he could dance. He remembered the steps. Rat's knees, the Wild West was fun!

CHAPTER 9

The Big Hoedown

"**Y**ou guys stole my idea," said Roger on the way back to the dining hall.

"What idea? Your dumb idea to be blind?" asked Tracy.

"It was my own idea to have a sprained ankle," said Molly. "I didn't steal it from anyone. Anyway, my ankle really hurt."

"All's well that ends well," said Patty. "That's what my grandma says. And it did end well. We had lots of fun learning to dance."

All the Pee Wees had to admit Patty was right.

"I wonder who will win the prize for best dancer," said Rachel. "I've been taking lessons for years, you know."

"Not in square dancing, you haven't," said Kenny. "Square dancing isn't like tap or ballet."

Rachel sighed. "A dancer is a dancer," she said. "If you have natural talent and grace you can do any dance."

Molly privately believed that square dancing took more listening and following directions than it did talent and grace. And Molly knew how to listen and follow directions. But of course she could never win anything after having just one lesson.

The Pee Wees were hungry after all their exercise. They had a big dinner in the dining hall. Then they went to the bunkhouse to get ready for the big dance. Mr. Peters was ironing the wrinkles out of the dance skirts and shirts. Mrs. Peters was braiding the girls' hair. She tied matching ribbons on ponytails that would bounce up and down while they danced.

When everyone was ready, they raced over to the big barn where the dance was to be held. Mr. Roscoe was there playing his fiddle. Colored lights were strung everywhere, and Chinese lanterns swung from the rafters. Chairs were set up all around the sides for people who did not want to dance.

But all the Pee Wees wanted to dance! They quickly got into their places when Mr. Roscoe called "Square up!" They prepared to do the steps as he called them out.

"Grab your partner, give her a whirl. Let's all do the California twirl!"

Molly listened very carefully to Mr. Roscoe. She found she had to really think hard to move so fast in the right direction.

Roger and Sonny were laughing and punching each other and stepping on each other's feet on purpose. When Mr. Roscoe called "Do-si-do," they walked the wrong way—right into the next square. They brought the whole dance to a stop.

"Let's all listen carefully to the calls," said Mr. Peters with a frown. "I think there's a little too much horseplay going on here."

Molly's partner was Kenny. He was a good listener. There was no horseplay in their square.

When the evening was half over, Molly's square was the only one that had made no mistakes.

But Molly was getting tired. Square dancing was very hard work. Especially when you were just learning. She didn't care about winning, she just wanted to do it right. It felt good to do something well!

There was a nice long break for refresh-

ments. The Pee Wees tumbled into chairs and drank some pink punch.

"Maybe when we get home, we can square-dance at our meetings. Right in your basement, Mrs. Peters," said Lisa.

"That's a good idea!" said their leader.

And then the break was over. Mr. Roscoe called, "Honor your partner, give her a swing. Allemande left, and weave that ring!"

"What a hoedown this is!" cried Andy. "Look at those Pee Wees dance!"

"Weave the ring, and Texas star. Half sashay just where you are," called Mr. Roscoe.

"Sides face! Grand square!" came next.

The grand square was hard! Molly knew she had to count her steps carefully. Kenny knew too. They carefully counted one, two, three as they moved. They turned on count four. One, two, three, *four*!

Sonny turned on count two. Ashley

turned on count three. But Molly and Kenny did it right.

Soon Mr. Roscoe called, "Promenade that partner home," and the dance was over. Molly noticed that her square was the only one still in place!

Rachel was graceful, but not fast.

Roger and Sonny were fast, but they didn't listen to directions.

Mary Beth's square was not square anymore. Tim had gotten his left side and right side mixed up. He had walked smack into Sonny, who had wandered across the room and into the wrong square. The two of them had landed in a pile on the floor.

But Kenny and Molly had promenaded home while everyone seated around the barn floor clapped and cheered.

Molly was very glad it was over! Her legs felt weak. Rat's knees, square dancing was good exercise!

"I'm really a ballerina," said Rachel, sitting down beside Molly. "Ballet is an art, you know."

"I'd have won if Sonny hadn't walked into me," said Tim.

"Hey! You walked into *me*!" shouted Sonny.

Mrs. Peters raised her hand. "I know you all worked hard tonight, and we all had a good time. But we have to give the prize to Molly and Kenny." She laughed. "They were the only ones left on the floor when it came time to promenade! They showed us how important it is to listen."

Most of the audience cheered, but a few Pee Wees booed. No one liked to lose. Molly and Kenny went up to get their prize. They each got a tiny fiddle to pin on their shirts. Molly couldn't wait to show her mom and dad!

"Now," said Cowboy Andy, "since it's our last night, it's time for the big sing-along!" He led the Pee Wees out of the barn. They walked down a path through the woods to a big clearing. In the clearing was the biggest bonfire Molly had ever seen! Bing was sitting near the fire, softly playing his guitar. As the Pee Wees sat down around the fire, the Moes and Bakers and Peterses brought them hot dogs and marshmallows on sticks to roast. Some of the Pee Wees dropped them into the fire by mistake and had to get new ones. Eventually everyone had their treats.

As they ate, Chip and Bing led them in song. Western songs and rounds and short songs and long songs. Everyone joined in. Even the Pee Wees who sang off-key. It was dark as could be in the woods. The only light was from the fire. It made flickering shadows on the Pee Wees' faces. Instead of being scary, thought Molly, it was peaceful. The Scouts' smiles, the crackling branches snapping in the fire, and the guitar music all made her feel warm and se-

cure. Molly wished it would last forever! But of course, it couldn't.

After all the excitement, it was hard to get to sleep that night. But finally the bunkhouse was quiet.

No one heard the coyotes howling in the distance.

No horseplay went on in the boys' bunkroom.

And there were no ghosts or other scary sounds in the night.

In the morning, it was time to say good-bye to the ranch and to Cowboy Andy. Good-bye to Chip. Good-bye to cowboy boots and ten-gallon hats.

"Come back again, you hear?" called Chip.

"We will!" called the Pee Wees, waving from inside their cars. They drove down the long driveway, past the Lazy T sign, and turned toward home.

"Andy said he'd write to me," said Ashley.

Mary Beth rolled her eyes at Molly. "I'll bet," she said. "I think she made that up."

"I think I'll ask for cowboy boots for Christmas," said Tracy.

Molly didn't want cowboy boots. She just wanted to keep her good memories, and her little fiddle, to remind her of the fun. And when they got back, she'd get a brand-new badge!

Rat's knees, Pee Wee Scouts was fun!

Pee Wee Scout Song
(to the tune of "Old MacDonald Had a Farm")

Scouts are helpers, Scouts have fun
Pee Wee, Pee Wee Scouts!
We sing and play when work is done,
Pee Wee, Pee Wee Scouts!

With a good deed here,
And an errand there,
Here a hand, there a hand,
Everywhere a good hand.

Scouts are helpers, Scouts have fun,
Pee Wee, Pee Wee Scouts!

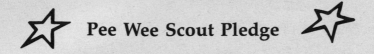 **Pee Wee Scout Pledge**

We love our country
And our home,
Our school and neighbors too.

As Pee Wee Scouts
We pledge our best
In everything we do.